THIS WALKER BOOK BELONGS TO:

_____

_____

_____

For Katherine and Robert at
College Farm

First published 1988 by Walker Books Ltd
87 Vauxhall Walk, London SE11 5HJ

This edition published 2002

2 4 6 8 10 9 7 5 3

This book has been typeset in Monotype Bembo

Printed in Hong Kong

British Library Cataloguing in Publication Data:
a catalogue record for this book is
available from the British Library

ISBN 0-7445-8923-1

QUACK QUACK

PATRICIA CASEY

WALKER BOOKS
AND SUBSIDIARIES
LONDON · BOSTON · SYDNEY

Out you go!

quack

quack

quack

Look in the shed.

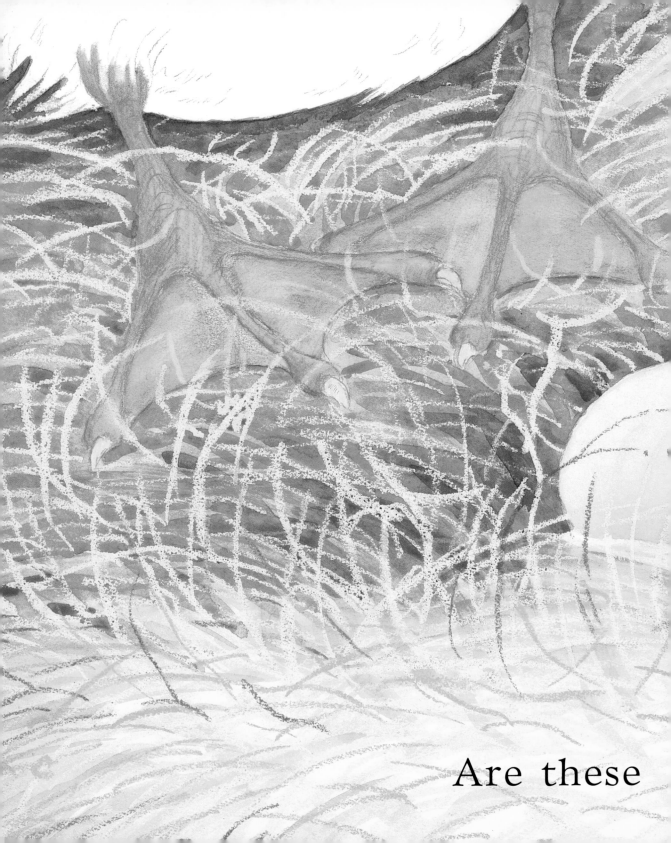

Are these

Duck's eggs?

Sit down.

cluck

QUACK

These are Hen's eggs!

Duck runs off for dinner.

Hen's eggs hatch.

Duck's eggs hatch.

cluck
cluck

quack
quack

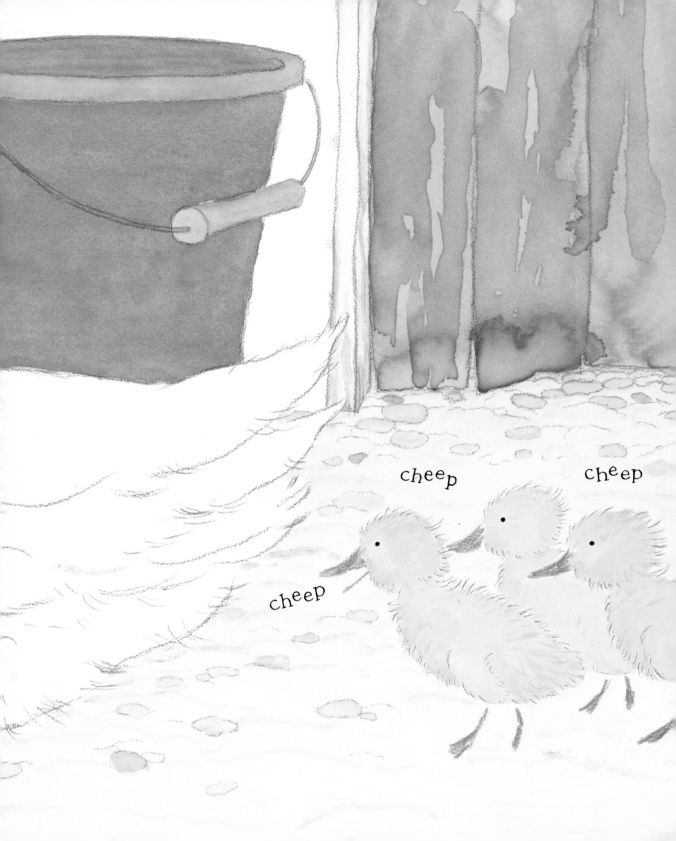

PATRICIA CASEY says of **Quack Quack**,
"I love watching and sketching the animals on the farm
and this little story happened right in front of my eyes."

Patricia Casey has illustrated natural history
subjects in numerous books for both adults and children.
Her titles for Walker include *The Best Thing About a Puppy*
by Judy Hindley; the Read and Wonder title *I Like
Monkeys Because…* by Peter Hansard; and her own books
Beep Beep! Oink Oink! Animals in the City and
One Day At Wood Green Animal Shelter.
Patricia lives in north London.

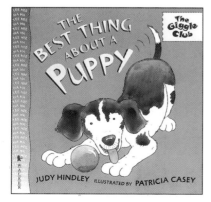

ISBN 0-7445-6085-3 (pb)

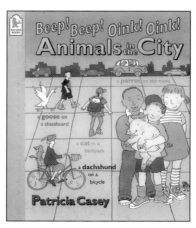

ISBN 0-7445-6341-0 (pb)

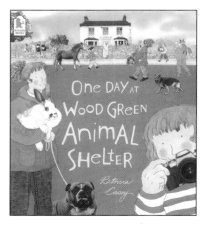

ISBN 0-7445-8928-2 (pb)